HOME
FOR A BUNNY

BY MARGARET WISE BROWN
PICTURES BY GARTH WILLIAMS

A GOLDEN BOOK • NEW YORK
Western Publishing Company, Inc., Racine, Wisconsin 53404

"Spring, Spring, Spring!"
sang the frog.
"Spring!"
said the groundhog.

"Spring, Spring, Spring!"
sang the robin.
It was Spring.
The leaves burst out.
The flowers burst out.
And robins burst out of their eggs.
It was Spring.

In the Spring a bunny
came down the road.
  He was going to find
a home of his own.
  A home for a bunny,
  A home of his own,
  Under a rock,
  Under a stone,
  Under a log,
  Or under the ground.
  Where would a bunny find a home?

"Where is your home?"
he asked the robin.

"Here, here, here,"
sang the robin.
"Here in this nest is my home."

"Here, here, here,"
sang the little robins
who were about to fall out of the nest.
"Here is our home."
"Not for me," said the bunny.
"I would fall out of a nest.
I would fall on the ground."

So he went on
looking for a home.
"Where is your home?"
he asked the frog.

"Wog, wog, wog,"
sang the frog.
"Wog, wog, wog,
Under the water,
Down in the bog."
"Not for me,"
said the bunny.
"Under the water,
I would drown in a bog."

So he went on
looking for a home.
"Where do you live?"
he asked the groundhog.
"In a log," said the groundhog.
"Can I come in?" said the bunny.
"No, you can't come in my log,"
said the groundhog.

So the bunny went down the road.
  Down the road
and down the road he went.
  He was going to find
a home of his own.
  A home for a bunny,
  A home of his own,
  Under a rock
  Or a log
  Or a stone.
  Where would a bunny find a home?

Down the road
and down the road
and down the road
he went, until—

He met a bunny.
"Where is your home?"
he asked the bunny.

"Here," said the bunny.
"Here is my home.
Under this rock,
Under this stone,
Down under the ground,
Here is my home."

"Can I come in?"
said the bunny.
"Yes," said the bunny.
And so he did.

And that was his home.